D0995445

Behold the secret headquarters of Superman.

The Fortress of Solitude contains a lab, a museum, a zoo of alien creatures and thousands of trophies from the Man of Steel's adventures.

In one corner, Superman safely keeps a starship from his home planet, Krypton. Here's the tale behind that artifact . . .

CHAPTER 1

HIDDEN FORTRESS

One bright morning, a red blur flashes over the Atlantic Ocean.

It is Superman, zooming towards the North Pole.

He carries a figure in his arms. She is wrapped in his cape.

"We're almost there, Lois," Superman tells the woman.

"My cape will keep you safe in this blizzard."

The cape also keeps Lois from seeing where Superman is flying.

Lois Lane, a reporter for the *Daily Planet* newspaper, is working on a story about the Man of Steel.

He has agreed to take her to his secret Fortress of Solitude.

Superman dives down from the clouds.

Seconds later, he and Lois stand at the icy entrance of the hideaway.

"This place is amazing!" says Lois, taking notes. "Are these souvenirs from your adventures?"

Superman nods.

"Clark will be so jealous that I got to cover this story," Lois says.

Clark Kent is her fellow reporter at the *Daily Planet*. Lois doesn't know that Clark Kent is secretly Superman.

Nor does she see a special memento Superman keeps hidden in a dark corner.

It is a small starship that saved the hero's life.

CHAPTER 2

DOOMED PLANET

Many years earlier . . .

A starship is being built on the planet
Krypton.

It is made by Jor-El and Lara, a husband and
wife who are famous scientists.

They work together in a hidden workshop.

Suddenly, the workshop trembles. The walls shake.

"Jor-El!" cries Lara. "The earthquakes are growing stronger!"

"We don't have much time," says Jor-El. "Quick – bring Kal-El here!"

Jor-El has discovered that Krypton is going to explode.

Everything on the planet will be destroyed.

So he and Lara had quickly built a starship.

They only had time to build a small one.

Lara carries a bundle towards the starship.

They place their son, Kal-El, inside the ship.

RUUMMMMMBLE!

The workshop trembles again.

"Goodbye, my son!" cries Lara.

"Earth will be his new home," says Jor-El.
"But he will always carry Krypton in his heart."

As the walls of the workshop crumble, the
starship rockets into space.

CHAPTER 3

VISITOR FROM SPACE

On Earth, an old pickup truck rambles between cornfields.

Jonathan and Martha Kent are driving home.

"I hope we beat the storm," says Jonathan.

"What's that?" cries Martha, stepping out of the truck.

She points to a streak of white stretching across the sky.

"Looks like a meteor," begins Jonathan.

BRRRUMMMMMMBLE

"Jonathan!" cries Martha. "It's an earthquake!

Jonathan steps on the brake.

"Not an earthquake," says Jonathan.

"That streak you saw in the sky," he says. "It landed over there."

In the cornfield, they see a long trench in the soil.

At the far end of the trench something lies buried in the ground.

"It looks like one of those spaceships from films," says Jonathan.

The buried object makes a humming sound.

Martha raises her head. "Is that thunder?" she whispers.

A metal door opens at the top of the object, and two small arms stick out.

They push up the metal lid.

"A child!" exclaims Martha.

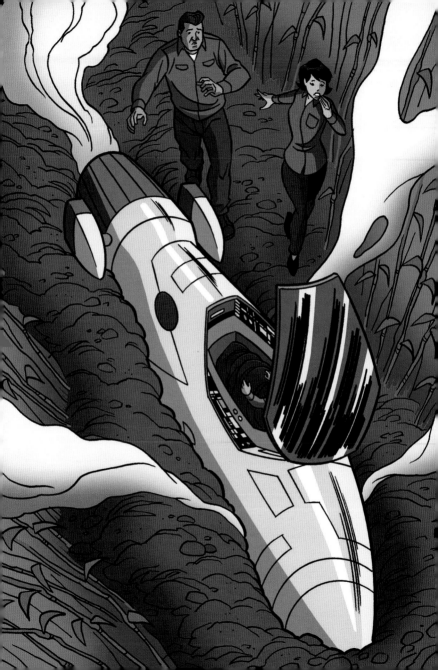

CHAPTER 4

DARK CLOUDS

Martha bends down and picks up the smiling toddler.

She turns to look at her husband.

"We always wanted a son," she says.

"But, Martha," Jonathan says. "What about his family? His parents?"

The woman looks down at the strange ship.

"I don't think they're from around here," she says.

The sky grows darker. Lightning flashes above the cornfields.

The child puts his arms around Martha's neck.

"Hurry, Jonathan! The storm's growing stronger," says Martha.

Her husband hitches the starship to the rear of his pickup truck.

"We better hide this in the barn," he says. "Don't want to get into any trouble."

CHAPTER 5

ANOTHER ESCAPE

Wind rocks the pickup truck.

The starship pulls against the chain.

"Quick, Martha," says Jonathan. "Get the kid inside!"

GRRRMMMMMMMM!

A rumbling sound grows louder and louder.

"What is that?" shouts Martha.

The ground shakes.

At the end of the road is a large, dark shape.

The windstorm has pushed over a silo from a nearby farm.

The giant metal tower is rolling straight towards the Kents' truck.

"Jonathan!" cries Martha.

The little toddler squirms out of Martha's arms.

She screams and lunges for the boy.

Too late! The little boy runs down the road, towards the deadly silo.

Martha and Jonathan rush after the boy.

The toddler sticks out his two small arms.

The silo rolls closer and closer.

The silo crashes onto the boy.

Suddenly, the boy lifts his arms and tosses the silo towards the cornfield.

The metal flies through the air.

The Kents hear it crashing far away.

Martha runs to the boy and lifts him into her arms.

Jonathan smiles and puts his arms around them both.

"I thought we were saving this little kid," he says. "But it looks like he's the one doing the saving."

"He's not a kid," says Martha Kent. "He's our son now.

"And his name is Clark."

EPILOGUE . . .

Lois Lane takes one last look around the Fortress of Solitude.

"Thanks for the tour, Superman," she says. "I'll have to tell Clark all about this."

Superman smiles and glances back at his favourite memento.

Clark knows all about this, thinks the Man of Steel. *Thanks to the starship from Krypton.*

GLOSSARY

hideaway secret place where someone can hide or hide things

Krypton Superman's home planet

memento small item kept to remember a place, an experience or a person

meteor piece of rock from space that enters Earth's atmospere at high speed, forming a streak of light in the sky

North Pole northernmost point on Earth

silo tall, round tower used to store food for farm animals

souvenir object kept to remind you of a person, place or event